Anansi:
An Unusual Experience

GILLENA COX

AuthorHouse™ UK
1663 Liberty Drive
Bloomington, IN 47403 USA
www.authorhouse.co.uk
Phone: 0800.197.4150

Published by AuthorHouse 03/14/2019

ISBN: 978-1-7283-8573-0 (sc)
ISBN: 978-1-7283-8574-7 (e)

Print information available on the last page.

authorHOUSE®

Introduction

Again, we meet The Anansi family. And again, it is Christmas
time. The spider/man Anansi is moody and brooding.
On this, particularly rainy Christmas morning.

Delightful reading hours to all

Dedication

To all lovers of Parang and 'nancy Stories

Contents

Chapter 1   Cinnamon Sticks 3

Chapter 2   A Giant Windy Hand 5

Chapter 3   On Camel Backs Three 7

Chapter 4   Where 9

Chapter 5   Sign Post 11

Chapter 6   From Air to Air 13

Chapter 7   Fried Bakes 15

Cinnamon Sticks

tinsel and baubles -
the sound of paper tearing
between giggles

And so it is; that rainy morning, the spidery Anansi, awakes to eight arms full of his two anansi children, tugging at him from every direction, pleading with him to come downstairs, to open a gift under the Christmas tree. He Anansi, never likes a rainy Christmas morning. He yawns and stretches, it is daylight and it is Christmas. Nevertheless, he gets out of bed to wishes of Merry Christmas.

Later that morning, left alone for a while, Anansi and Mrs. Anansi sit at the table sipping coffee. They use cinnamon sticks to stir, stirring slowly. They sip and they talk, for the children are too excited by their new toys to feel hungry, or even remember, they have anansi parents.

However, still later in the day, when they gather, for a late Christmas lunch, it is then, that Anansi, in between mouthfuls of green fig salad, decides to relate this experience.

A Giant Windy Hand

a ruffle of drapes -
sound of windchimes
they tinkle sweetly

The night before; in between a patter and splash of raindrops on the pavement, there arose an unusual wind. Which, not content to only ruffle Mrs. Anansi's pretty new drapes, she ruffles and weaves herself into the Anansi house, winding her way up the Anansi staircase, into the Anansi bedrooms, peering here, and peering there, until at last, reaching the room shared by Anansi and his charming wife. Here, this unusual gust, shapes herself into a giant windy hand, large enough to pick up an unsuspecting, Anansi, leaving behind, Mrs. Anansi asleep.

"Come with me Anansi" says the unusual Wind, "I will take you on a little trip." Poor Anansi, he is terrified. Yet still, he clutches Wind's giant hand and off they go swoooosh into the night. Anansi thinks to himself, this must be exactly how great Moon feels in all her waning and waxing shapes. There, suspended in the night sky, he thinks he even saw an unusually bright star in passing.

On Camel Backs Three

they travel afar –
gold frankincense and myrrh
their gifts of reverence

Tossed, swivelled and swirled, Anansi is so terrified, he cannot even feel air sick. This great Spider/Man Anansi, who can at a whim, weave amazing webs. He peers through the night; thick and dark, to see what he could see.

There they are. Far down below, three unusually dressed men riding on the backs of camels, carrying gifts of some sort. They sit so regally in the desert of falling snowflakes. Not even once brushing away a snowflake. Snowflakes in the desert? You might ask. Yes, snowflakes in the desert. It is you must remember, an unusual night. Some even call it a Holy night.

Anansi thinks, how wise these three men are. Sitting on the backs of camels holding their packages ever so tightly, ever so securely. They seem to be travelling very far into the night. And their camels stride happily, nonetheless. They do not even look tired.

Where

wind in the trees –
silhouettes dancing in
a joyous night

Anansi is enthralled. He stares, his spidery mouth wide open in amazement. "But where are they going, just the three of them? There is no one else about, and at this very late hour of the night. Don't they have families? Wives to help with shelling of pigeon peas? Children's gifts to wrap? Ham to bake for the Paranderos when they visit?"

As he asked these questions of Wind, with each question, his mood softens, and his spidery face brightens. "Where are we Anansi asks again?" Wind however had spoken her bit for that night, when she had commanded: "Come with me Anansi."

And so, to Anansi's questions now, she gives no reply. It is just swoosh, after swoosh, after swoosh. As wind goes this way and that, carrying poor Anansi in her grasp. Anansi, he who could spin fabulous webs, was caught securely in Wind's grasp helpless.

Sign Post

twinkle of stars –
somewhere in a manger
a baby sleeps

Anansi, from trillions of night clouds above, cranes his neck this way and that. He thinks he saw a sign. Then. Yes, it is! A neon sign which reads Bethlehem Ephrathah – Stable, about 2 to 3 swoooshes away.

Gently, gently, gently Anansi is nearing the ground. Then Wind, opens slightly, the door to a stable. No one looked around. The door is opened so quietly; and it is there, Anansi sees: ox, donkey, sheep, cattle. All present; serenely, in the sweet hay. Some munching and some not.

The same three unusually dressed men are presenting gifts to... and this is when Anansi squeals with delight "baby Jesus and Mary and Joseph, shepherds and Little Drummer Boy!" Anansi claps his hands for joy and does a happy dance, but no one looks around. No one sees or hears Anansi; but everyone hears angels singing, "Joy to the world let earth receive her King."

From Air to Air

asleep in a trough
this adorable baby –
songs of angels

It is indeed, a night so Holy. What a wonderous feeling. "Wind, thank you for lifting my spirits, thank you for taking me back to the true meaning of Christmas" says a humbled happy Anansi, smiling from air to air.

There is no response from Wind. Anansi looks around trying to find Wind. "Wind, Winnnd, Winnnnd", but there is no Wind. Only, a very contented Anansi. A coolness, a feeling of joy, and a stable full of warmth and peace and love. All lit up in the glow of a wonderous, unusually bright star.

A star with a tail, extending into the deep inky dark sky. A tail which reminds Anansi of flying kites with his children in the Queens Park Savannah on a bright sunny day. Kites, high above blooming Poui trees some with pink flowers and some with brilliant yellow flowers.

Fried Bakes

drenching hearts of every Scrooge
a downpour Christmas morning

Well, like I said before; and I am saying again, it was an unusually rainy December, when, Anansi awoke one morning in a rather dull lethargic mood. For he never liked rainy Christmases.

Anyways; there was nothing unusual in the family kitchen (in the tropical island of Trinidad), in which cooking oil slowed to an eerie hot stillness in a large frying pot (even though it was raining outside), into which the radiant Mrs Anansi was dropping, evenly formed bits of white flour dough, making fried bakes, on that particular Christmas morning. And he, Anansi, had to lose his grumpiness and get out of bed even though it was raining. He just did not like rain on Christmas morning.

And this is how that Christmas day started.

THE END

Wishes for a Merry Christmas And a Bright and
Prosperous New Year, dear readers.

Some Words Explained

Green Figs - green Bananas, in the Caribbean used for cooking. [making curries, salads, and such like.]

Fried Bakes - tiny bits of dough; flattened and deep fried.

Haibun – a Japanese literary form including prose and haiku.

Haiku - Plural also haiku. Therefore: one haiku, two haiku. A very tiny poem of Japanese origin. Presented in one to three lines, of not more than seventeen syllables. Generally, it records a moment in nature.

Paranderos – singers of Parang a form of Christmas music in Trinidad and Tobago.

Poui - a flowering tree; (genus or scientific name, Tabebuia).

ABOUT THE AUTHOR

Gillena Cox Lives in St James, Trinidad of The Republic of Trinidad and Tobago. A retired Library Assistant. Amateur writer and photographer; dabbling in poetry and children's stories, nature photos, and as well blogging, writing and interacting within online poet communities – her hobbies.

Born 1950. Married in 1971. A mother and grandmother.

Favourite Casual Wear – Jeans, Tee Shirt and Sandals

OTHER BOOKS BY
THIS AUTHOR

Moments – 100 haiku poems 2007 [Adult]

Pink Crush – a book of poems 2011 [Adult]

The Little Seed and His Brother 2015 [Children]

Under the Chinaberry Tree 2016 [Children]

Third Planet from The Sun 2017 [Children]

Anansi and the Twelve Days of Christmas 2018 [Children/ Chapter book]